March 24, 2018

Dearest Dominik, Sebastian & Isabella,
Thank you for being sparkler
in my day - Lucky Me !

Love,
Lara

# LUCKY ME

by Lora Rozler • Illustrations by Jan Dolby

Published in Canada by Fitzhenry & Whiteside
195 Allstate Parkway, Markham, ON   L3R 4T8
Published in the United States by Fitzhenry & Whiteside
311 Washington Street, Brighton, MA   02135


10 9 8 7 6 5 4 3 2 1

Fitzhenry & Whiteside acknowledges with thanks the Canada Council for the Arts and the Ontario Arts Council for their support of our publishing program.
We acknowledge the financial support of the Government of Canada through the Canada Book Fund (CBF) for our publishing activities.

Canada Council    Conseil des Arts
for the Arts      du Canada

ONTARIO ARTS COUNCIL
CONSEIL DES ARTS DE L'ONTARIO
an Ontario government agency
un organisme du gouvernement de l'Ontario

Library and Archives Canada Cataloguing in Publication
Rozler, Lora, 1977-, author
Lucky me / by Lora Rozler ; illustrations by Jan Dolby.


ISBN 978-1-55455-410-2 (hardcover)


1. Gratitude--Juvenile literature.  2. Etiquette for children
and teenagers--Juvenile literature.  3. Vocabulary--Juvenile
literature.  I. Dolby, Jan, 1967-, illustrator  II. Title.


BJ1533.G8R69 2017          j179'.9          C2017-905446-5


Publisher Cataloging-in-Publication Data (U.S.)


Names: Rozler, Lora, 1977-, author. | Dolby, Jan, illustrator.
Title: Lucky Me / by Lora Rozler ; illustrations by Jan Dolby.
Description: Markham, Ontario : Fitzhenry & Whiteside, 2017.| Summary: "Lucky Me shows young readers how to say and learn
"Thank You" in many languages/cultures found across this diverse world" – Provided by publisher.
Identifiers: ISBN 978-1-55455-410-2 (hardcover)
Subjects: LCSH: Gratitude – Juvenile fiction. | Language and languages—Foreign words and phrases – Juvenile fiction.
BISAC: JUVENILE FICTION / Social Themes / Emotions & Feelings. | JUVENILE FICTION / People & Places / General.
Classification: LCC PZ7.1R695Lu |DDC [E] – dc23


Text and cover design by Kerry Plumley
Printed in Hong Kong by Sheck Wah Tong

For my Mom and Dad, who've always been my lucky stars.
A million times, *thank you!*
Lora Rozler

For Kenny. I'm thankful for our friendship.
Jan Dolby

I thank my lucky star for treasures,
big and small. I'm grateful each day,
thank you.
English

For the questions
that fuel my mind,
shnorhakalut'yun (shur-nur-ah-gah-lem).
Armenian

For warm and tasty
pancakes,
multumesc (mul-tsu-mesk).
Romanian

For sidewalk masterpieces,
efharisto (ef-har-rih-stowe).
Greek

For adventures in the
playground,
arigato (ahree-gah-tow).
Japanese

For a moustache
just like grandpa's,
salamat (sa-la-maht).
Tagalog

For a princess
crowned a hero,
toda (toh-da).
Hebrew

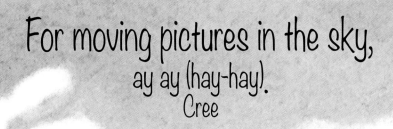

For moving pictures in the sky,
ay ay (hay-hay).
Cree

For coasters, clowns
and funnel cake,
gracias (gra-see-us).
Spanish

For built-in playmates,
obrigado (oh-bree-gah-doh).
Portuguese

For ice-cream in
a heat wave,
mahadsanid (ma-had sa-nid).
Somali

For ABCs and 123s,
xie xie (syeh-syeh).
Mandarin

For tea parties with
The Queen,
dank je (dank-ya).
Dutch

For earth and
all its beauty,
kiitos (key-tose).
Finnish

For buttery popcorn in the dark,
dziekuje (dsyen-koo-yeh).
Polish

For boo-boo fixes
and soothing words,
shukran (shoe-krahn).
Arabic

For another candle
on my cake,
dhanyavad (dha-nya-vaad).
Hindi

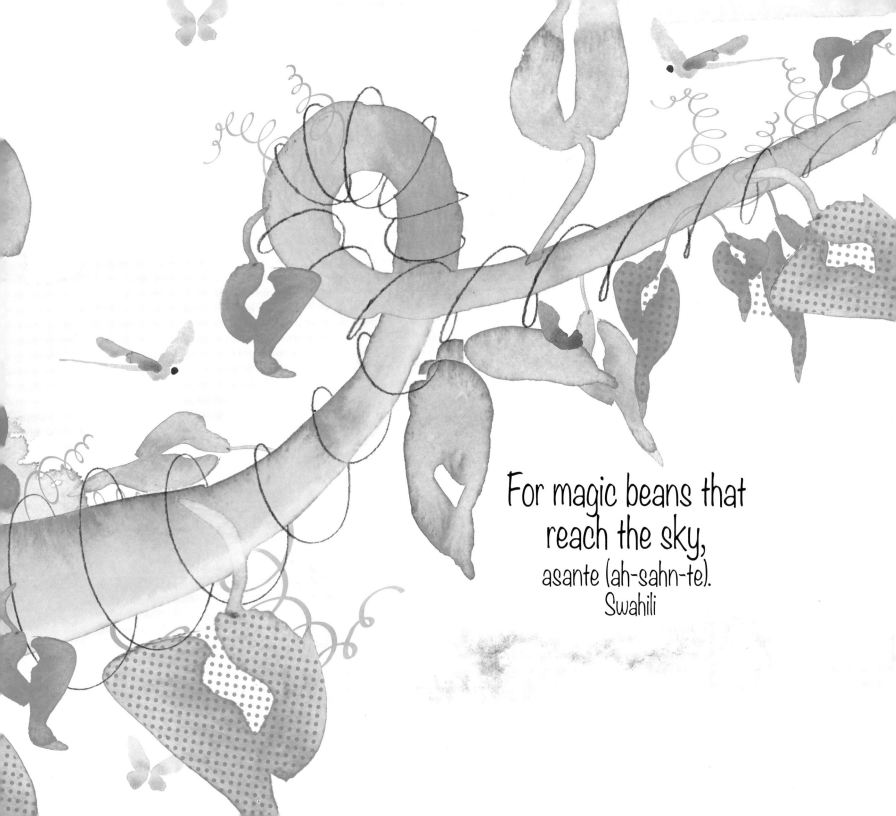

For magic beans that
reach the sky,
asante (ah-sahn-te).
Swahili

For snowmen made anew each year,
nandri (nun-dree).
Tamil

For my sidekicks when I need them,
cam on (gahm-uhn).
Vietnamese

For angels in the snow,
gamsahabnida (gam-sah-hab-nee-da).
Korean

For spooky tales by firelight,
koszonom (kus-zun-um).
Hungarian

For mud pies and spaghetti worms,
spasiba (spa-see-bah).
Russian

For the sand
beneath my toes,
faleminderit (fah-leh-mee-ndeh-reet).
Albanian

For the waves that nearly catch me,
grazie (graht-see).
Italian

For concerts
in the kitchen,
mamnunam, (mam-noon-am).
Persian

For monster's caves
and lurking bears,
do jeh (daw-dyeh).
Cantonese

For the wonders of creation,
meherbani (mi-har-baan-ee).
Punjabi

For a place to rest my head as
I drift to faraway kingdoms,
danke (dahn-kah).
German

For road trip sing-alongs,
teshekkur (the-sheh-kur).
Turkish

For daylight's tickle
on my nose,
shukriya (shoo-kree-a).
Urdu

I thank my lucky star for treasures,
old and new. I'm grateful for each day,
Merci pour tout!
French